Teenage Refugees From

MEXICO

Speak Out

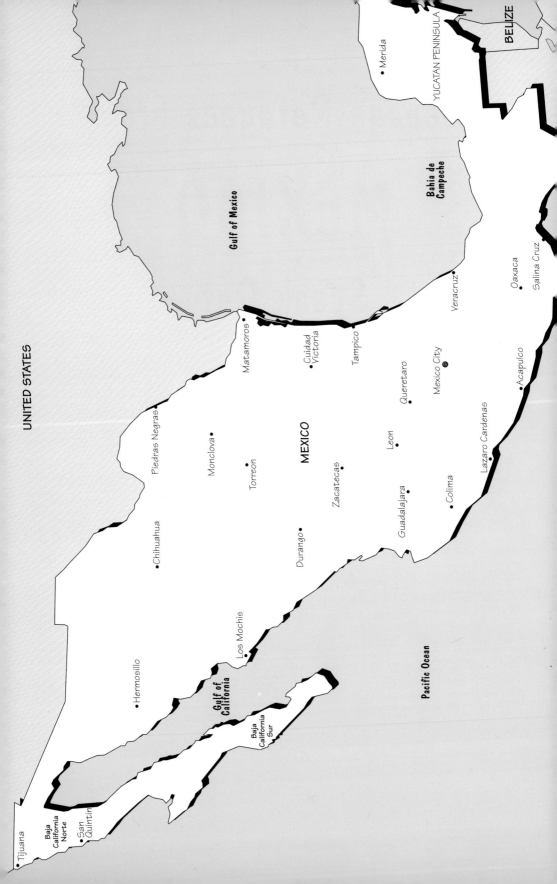

IN THEIR OWN VOICES

Teenage Refugees From

MEXICO

Speak Out

GERRY HADDEN

THE ROSEN PUBLISHING GROUP, INC.
NEW YORK

Published in 1997 by The Rosen Publishing Group, Inc.
29 East 21st Street, New York, NY 10010

First Edition
Copyright © 1997 by The Rosen Publishing Group, Inc.

Library of Congress Cataloging-in-Publication Data

Teenage refugees from Mexico speak out / [compiled by] Gerry Hadden. —
   1st ed.
       p.   cm. — (In their own voices)
   Includes bibliographical references and index.
   Summary: Six teenagers tell about their experiences in immigrating to the
United States for the opportunities which elude them in Mexico because of
its political and economic instability.
   ISBN 0-8239-2441-6
   1. Mexican American teenagers—Juvenile literature.   2. Refugees—
United States—Juvenile literature.   [1. Mexican Americans.
2. Refugees.   3. Youths' writings.]   I. Hadden, Gerry.   II. Series.
E184.M5T44 1997
973'.046872073—dc21   96-38914
                                                                        CIP
                                                                         AC

Manufactured in the United States of America.

Contents

Moises Tejeda lowers a rack of tobacco at his job on a farm in Virginia. Many recent Mexican immigrants work long hours in low-paying jobs.

INTRODUCTION

Some say Latin America's greatest challenge is making its economies and governments as healthy as its rich cultures and religions. So far, many Latin American countries have come close to achieving stability and prosperity, only to falter and regress. Nowhere is this more true than in Mexico. Because of this, many Mexicans come, or try to come, to the United States every year.

For more than 500 years, Mexico has maintained strong cultural and spiritual ties to Spain, a country that at one time controlled most of Latin America. Before the arrival of the Spaniards on Mexican soil, the land was inhabited by Indian peoples, descendants of Asian nomads

7

The Mayan ruins at Chichén Itzá are an example of the many accomplishments of Mexico's indigenous people.

who crossed the Bering Strait to the North American continent. With the development of agriculture in approximately 7000 BC, Mexican Indian society began to transform itself. Complex and sophisticated civilizations emerged. By 600 AD, the city of Teotihuacán in central Mexico boasted pyramids, broad avenues, and temples. It became a bustling population center.

The Mayan civilization in Mexico's Yucatán Peninsula provides another example of amazing achievements of early peoples. The Mayans developed a writing system, advanced mathematics, astronomy, and innovative agricultural and medical techniques. The ancient city of Chichén Itzá,

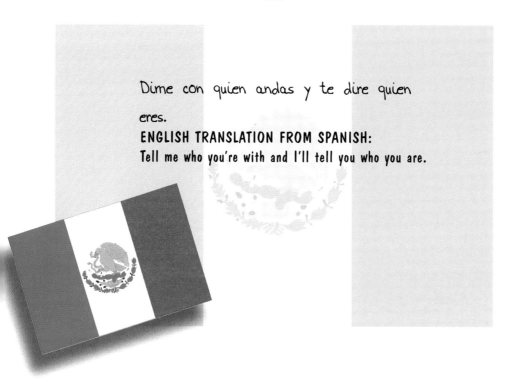

Dime con quien andas y te dire quien eres.

ENGLISH TRANSLATION FROM SPANISH:
Tell me who you're with and I'll tell you who you are.

located in the central Yucatán, was probably founded by the Itzá, a Mayan people who resisted attempts by the Spanish to convert and defeat them. Palenque in Chiapas, Mexico, was another great Mayan city. Today, large numbers of people on Mexico's Yucatán Peninsula are Mayan.

The Toltec and Aztec empires further contributed to the development of Mexican society and culture. After the Aztecs were defeated by the Spanish in 1521, increasing numbers of Spaniards and enslaved Africans began to arrive in Mexico. The period of Spanish colonial rule in Mexico was a grim one for Indian peoples. They were forced to work as slaves in gold and silver mines and were exposed to deadly European diseases.

Mexico finally achieved independence from Spain in 1821. In honor of the Aztecs, to whom the eagle and the serpent were sacred, Mexico's new government chose these symbols to represent their new country on the national flag.

Ironically, many of the Mexicans who immigrate to the United States come to areas that were once part of Mexico. When Mexico gained its independence from Spain, its territory included what are today the states of California, Nevada, Utah, Arizona, New Mexico, Texas, and parts of Colorado and Wyoming. This land was lost by Mexico in the U.S.-Mexican War (1846–1848).

Contemporary Mexican society is made up of dozens of ethnic groups of Indian, European, and African descent. The Mexican government has estimated that approximately 80 percent of the Mexican population is *mestizo* —that is, of mixed Spanish and Indian descent.

Mexican immigration to the United States is not a new phenomenon. Throughout the two countries' shared history, the United States has been viewed by many Mexicans as a place offering better education, jobs, improved living conditions, and a stable democracy. Between 1910 and 1920, thousands of Mexicans came to the United States to escape the chaos of the Mexican Revolution. The 1980s were also a

Two Mexican citizens relax on the beach in Tijuana, Mexico, as construction continues on extending the border fence into the Pacific Ocean.

period of increased emigration from Mexico, as the nation was hit by inflation and political instability. A drop in world oil prices in the 1980s caused an economic crisis for Mexico, one of the world's largest oil producers. Earthquakes that hit Mexico in 1985 killed thousands and caused billions of dollars in damage. These disasters drove many Mexicans to seek better fortunes in the United States.

Mexico, as a nation, faces many tough questions today. Why does this country, so rich in traditions and natural resources, with such varied and beautiful landscapes and such a diversity of people, still lag behind other countries politically and economically? What has kept Mexico from 11

The late César Chávez fought for better working conditions for Mexican migrant workers. As the leader of the United Farm Workers, Chávez organized a grape boycott to protest the use of toxic pesticides. Above, Chávez leads a rally in New York City in 1986.

fully adopting democratic principles and taking advantage of its economic potential? Are these problems the result of hundreds of years of colonialism? Will things change, in this era of free trade between Canada, Mexico, and the United States, or will the United States' southern neighbor remain in relative poverty?

These are difficult questions. They strike at the roots of the Mexican experience and are not easily answered. But addressing them may help us understand why so many Mexicans continue to leave their homeland—legally and illegally—to begin new lives in the United States.

13

The United States does not grant official refugee status to Mexican citizens. Yet in most of Mexico, economic and social conditions make it very difficult to survive. Though North America's borders were opened to trade in 1994 with the passage of the North American Free Trade Agreement (NAFTA), so far life has not improved for the average Mexican. Unemployment is rampant. The value of the Mexican currency, the *peso*, is very low. At the same time, the United States has tightened security along the Mexican border. The United States hopes to reduce the number of illegal immigrants trying to find a way into this country from Mexico and other Latin American countries. Despite these efforts, thousands of Mexicans enter the United States every year. Many use the help of "coyotes," or people who help immigrants cross the border into the United States illegally.

Mexico's record on human rights is less than perfect. The human rights monitoring organization Human Rights Watch found problems with the fairness of Mexico's 1994 elections, citing cases of fraud and attacks on election workers. Human Rights Watch reported that the Mexican army has also violated human rights in its response to the presence of armed rebels in the Mexican state of Chiapas. Following an uprising by the rebels in 1994, the Mexican army reportedly made sweeps of many towns and villages, killing, injuring, and arresting many civilians.

Those arrested were sometimes held for long periods and tortured. Mexico's president, Ernesto Zedillo Ponce de Leon, has publicly acknowledged that police officers, soldiers, and others are often not brought to justice for violating human rights.

Amnesty International, another organization concerned with human rights, reports that Mexican women in particular are often the targets of human rights violations. Indigenous women and women who work as human rights activists are especially vulnerable.

Mexicans who manage to flee across the border are not always safe from human rights abuses, either. U.S. border patrol agents along the border between the United States and Mexico have been accused in some cases of shooting, raping, and beating individuals trying to enter the United States. Victims of such abuses face many obstacles in filing complaints.

Once in the United States, Mexican immigrants often work long, hard hours at low-paying jobs to support themselves and their families. Many send a portion of their earnings back to Mexico to support other family members. Employers often take advantage of illegal immigrants, knowing that the immigrants will not report unfair treatment or poor working conditions because they fear being sent back to Mexico.

Most of the teenagers who tell their stories in this book can attend public school in the United

States because the U.S. law states that public schools cannot deny education to children whether they are citizens or not. But once high school is over, only U.S. citizens can go to college because identification and proof of residency are required. As you will see, this presents a big dilemma for immigrant students who aspire to higher education.

Because several of the teens in this book are illegal immigrants, they did not want their photos to be used in case they are recognized and sent back to Mexico.

In this book, young Mexicans talk about their experiences entering the United States. Here they try to adapt to a new country and its different customs, beliefs, and expectations. Some of their stories are hopeful, some tragic. Yet each student has been willing to endure his or her hardships in the name of one idea: opportunity.◆

Diego has had a very difficult life. He wants to finish his education but cannot attend school right now because he must work to support himself. He lives in Portland, Oregon.

DIEGO
I FEEL MORE FREE

My name is Diego. I come from Guadalajara, the capital of the state of Jalisco. I'm twenty years old. I haven't finished high school yet. Right now I'm not in school because I'm living with my brother, and I have to work to help pay the rent. Actually I haven't worked in three weeks. I'm looking for something, but since I'm here illegally, I don't have a green card. It is hard to get a job without the proper papers.

I came here because I had many problems at home. My problems were both personal and financial. It's hard for me to talk about it.

I never speak with my parents. Because of the problems I experienced during my childhood, I don't speak to my mother. Last Christmas my brother spoke with her, but I couldn't. I still wasn't ready. Finally, though, I did. I don't put all the blame on her. But I still haven't spoken with my father.

I blame my father for all of our problems. When he met my mother, he began a relationship with her before getting married. Her parents found out and said, "You have to get married." So he married her. But he never wanted to.

When my two oldest sisters were very young, my father began to abuse them. As they grew up and started bringing boyfriends home, my father would hit my sisters. He didn't want them dating anyone. He was jealous. As a result, both of my sisters married at sixteen, just to get away from our father.

My father began abusing one of my brothers. But my other brother wouldn't let him. Before all of this, one of my sisters tried to get our mother to separate from our father, but it never happened. As I grew up, my father would chase me from the house all the time. He said all his sons had to work for him, bringing him money. I'm not angry at my father anymore, but I don't want to talk to him. He has a sickness in his heart.

I crossed into the United States at the Tijuana border in the middle of the night, just like almost everyone else who comes to the United States from the south. It was in August, two years ago. I crossed with two friends. In Tijuana we found

This freeway sign in California's San Diego County warns motorists about illegal aliens who run across the border from Mexico.

a "coyote." We each paid $300 to cross the border. These coyotes have friends or relatives in the United States who help them. They want to know who will pay for the crossing. My brother paid for me. I crossed in a truck, hidden behind one of its walls. The space was only four feet high and very narrow.

After you cross the border, you have to wait until the coyote tells you to come out. Then you run. You have to cross the Rio Grande. There are places where it's shallow enough to wade across. As we crossed, I saw the police passing by very close. They were coming toward us, but they saw this other couple nearby who were crossing at the same time. The man tried to run, and the police chased after him. They were crossing with drugs. That left me free, and I made it without a problem.

Once in the United States, I spent about fifteen days in California. It was a horrible place. I didn't have any friends or relatives there. I thought my people, other Mexicans, would be more friendly to me, but they weren't because they didn't know me. I had to spend fifteen days there waiting for my brother to come get me. He has a wife and small boy. We all went up to his home in Portland, Oregon, together. Now my brother and his wife are separated. I don't see her much.

I was in school more than half a year, but I was living with my brother and his wife, and she

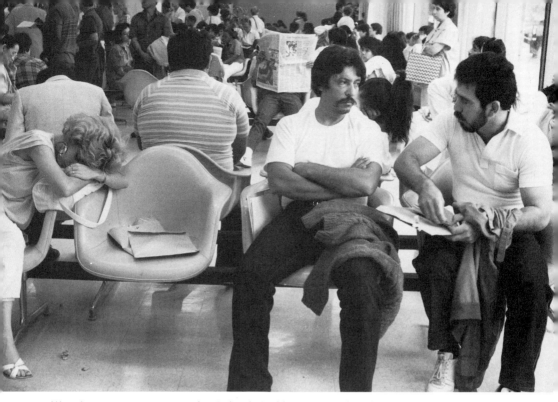

Illegal immigrants wait at the Federal Building in Los Angeles to file applications to begin the process of becoming legal immigrants.

began making problems for me. I didn't like her very much. Eventually she threw me out of the house. My brother ended up taking her side. He told me to just wait a little while and in the meantime learn some English so I could find work. I accepted this, and later my brother and his wife separated. After that I returned and helped my brother with the rent. I used to work in a deli but now I'm unemployed again.

I liked school in the United States a lot. But I had to leave because my brother would not support me. He said I had to help with the rent because he couldn't handle it alone. The whole time I was in school, he was paying the rent for both of us. He also had to pay for the car insurance and for child support for his son.

I went to a local Latino community center for help, but they didn't treat me very well. They were giving more help to other Americans, not to Mexicans.

Finally I got a job working for a beauty-supply company. I made enough to pay my share of everything. Right now my brother and his wife are trying to work out their problems. She might come back soon. If she comes back, I'll have to leave again. She and I can't live together. The problem, really, is that my brother and I don't understand each other very well. It has a lot to do with our childhood. He came to the United States five years ago, and after he got here he never called us in Mexico. I lost almost all contact with him. Sometimes he spoke to my mother, but never with me. Before he left we were really good friends. We did everything together. When he left I was still a boy. But when I arrived I was a grown-up, and we've had to get to know each other all over again. I have four other brothers and five sisters. Two of my brothers are here in the United States.

My life is full of problems. On the outside I may seem happy, but inside I'm not at all. One of my brothers here is a teacher. But he went to jail for using drugs. My whole family has broken up because of the problems we had as kids.

Right now I don't want to return to Mexico.

But the problem is that I'm here illegally. People have told me I should marry an American girl, because it's the only way to get a green card. That's how my brother did it.

If I had a lot of money, I could do whatever I wanted. I would study computers. I have great grades in math. A neighbor of mine has a computer, and he's teaching me how to use it. If I had a career in computers, I would return to my country and earn a lot of money.

Luckily my parents are now separated, living in separate houses. My mom lives with my two youngest sisters. My dad lives alone now. I'm happier now that I'm here. There are good things and bad things about living here. I have my friends. I feel more free.

Right now, I'm just looking for work and a girlfriend. I've had American girlfriends before, but I haven't met the right one yet.

American people seem very strange to me. For example, if someone is living on the street, the people here never stop to think about whether that person is cold. They don't think about why they came to this country to begin with. Americans don't realize that everyone comes here for the same reason: to have a better life.◆

Patricia is finishing her last year of high school. She and her family immigrated to the United States legally. She is looking forward to exploring the career opportunities in the United States that would not be available to her as a woman in Mexico.

PATRICIA
TOGETHER AS A FAMILY

My name is Patricia. I'm twenty years old. I'm a senior in high school. I should be a junior, but I have to finish before I'm twenty-one. I'm taking seven classes right now in school, and one after school—U.S. history. I want to study computers or medicine. I hope that after I learn more English in community college, I'll go to a university.

All of my brothers and sisters are doing well in school here. My youngest brother has a 4.0 grade point average in middle school. The problem is that we only came here with visiting papers, so entering college will be very difficult. I've spoken to many people at various colleges and universities, and they've all told me that without a green card I can't apply for any classes or scholarships or anything. And I have a 3.9 grade point average. I'm hoping to receive my papers in the next few months so I can attend college. I've been in the United States two and a half years.

We didn't have a big problem coming here. My father came here first, and then the rest of us came a few years later. If you have an education, you can apply for a visitor's visa to the United States. They ask you lots of questions, including how much money you have. But if you're really poor, there's no way you'll get a visa. That's why all those people are forced to cross the border illegally.

My main hobby is dancing. I take many dance classes. I'm not twenty-one, but if I go to the clubs early for dinner I can stay and dance later. I also love listening to music. I don't like most American music. But I love Mariah Carey. She has a beautiful voice.

I don't go out that much because my father is pretty conservative. I can go out if I really want to, but if I do, he won't speak to me for a while. I'm not grounded, but he gets his point across. If I go with my brother Arturo, then it's fine. My father knows Arturo will take care of me.

Our family is Catholic, and we go to church every Sunday. In Mexico we went daily, in the

Arthur Holmes, a science teacher, discusses the ocean with his class of Mexican
immigrant children near Charleston, South Carolina.

evening. I teach Sunday school here. I love it. But I don't want to be a teacher as a career. I don't think I have the patience for it!

When we came to the United States, we flew from Mexico to California to stay with my uncle. Then we drove to Seattle. I like Seattle a lot, but it took me quite a while to adjust to life here. Now I feel much better. In the beginning, I didn't want to get used to life here. But I didn't want to return to Mexico either, mostly because my dad is here, and I don't want to be separated from him. It's easier to deal with life's problems together as a family.

People here think differently. Where I lived is called Canana de Caracheo. It is a very small place. It's not even on the map. Everyone there has cows. It's like a ranch. As a woman in this place I couldn't study. You can only cook and clean. Women aren't permitted to get an education, only the men. In the United States I can do so much more. For example, I can work and study and not be totally dependent on a man.

Until ninth grade I wanted to study cosmetology. But I stopped studying because my parents felt I should learn the "proper" work of a woman, which is cooking and cleaning. So I went and worked for the priest at our church. I cooked, cleaned, and did secretarial work for him. I liked it a lot. But after just two months we came here.

My friends here are American, Japanese, and Guatemalan. I have friends from everywhere. I

A man sits down to eat a meal provided by Catholic missionaries in Tijuana. The missionaries provide hot meals and a place to stay for people on their way to the United States, or for people who were turned back by U.S. immigration officers.

A young girl looks after her family's flock of goats and sheep near Ixmiquilpan, Mexico.

don't care about nationalities. Sometimes I've encountered some racism here, but I don't pay any attention to it. For instance, I had one teacher who was unfair with my homework. Once I made one mistake, and she gave me a C. I asked her why, and she took my papers and just threw them in the garbage. I compared it to my friends' papers. Mine had fewer mistakes, but that didn't seem to matter. I've had many problems with this person. The director of the ESL (English as a Second Language) program had a meeting with this person, and now it's better. She's a good teacher, but I think she has something against Mexicans.

   One thing I can't get used to is that if you have a boyfriend here, after one week he wants to become very intimate with you. I don't like this. It's too fast. American boys want to move very quickly.

In Mexico, I went to a high school run by nuns. The school was very strict about everything.

We were a middle-class family in Mexico. My father owned a trucking business. But we had to spend all of our savings to keep the trucks in good repair. My mother worked in a restaurant making food. Life is much easier now that we're together again. I miss home, but my family is the most important thing to me.

My boyfriend here is Mexican, but he's been here so long he barely speaks Spanish. Most American students don't know too much about Mexico, especially about where I come from. Some are curious about where I used to live, but most don't ask.

Even though we have free trade with the United States and Canada, I don't think life will change very much for my country. Prices will rise as people earn more money, so things will stay the same.

One great thing about the United States is that I've been exposed to so many people from different countries that I never even knew about before I came here. And I've learned that even though everyone's faces are different, we're really all the same.◆

Arturo is Patricia's younger brother. Like her, he has a passion for dancing and is an excellent student.

ARTURO
I'LL NEVER STOP DANCING

'm sixteen years old. My father's already been here for five years. When he moved to the United States, we were still in Mexico. He moved to the United States because we were having some financial problems at home. We're much better off here. These days my father works in a barrel factory.

I came here with my mother, two brothers, and two sisters. I'm the second oldest. Life here is very different. Back in Mexico I spent a lot of time preparing for high school every day. I wanted to be a businessman. There weren't any schools for this near my house. I traveled an hour each way every day just to take my classes. I had a truck in Mexico; it was my uncle's, and

A worker unloads boxes of grapes during the grape harvest in California.

that's how I got to school. I have two uncles and a grandmother here. They've been here about thirteen years.

In Mexico my mom was a housewife, and my dad was a truck driver. My dad's job didn't pay a lot. Also, from sitting so much in the truck, he was hurting his legs. He needed to get up and move around more. He sold his trucks and moved to California.

When he first arrived in California, he worked with my two uncles in a factory packing tomatoes. He didn't like it very much because he had to work at night. It was very hard for him to adjust to his new schedule. So he moved to Seattle and started working in the barrel factory. My mom is still a housewife.

I'm still not entirely sure what I want to do in the future. But I still have time. My immediate plans are to finish high school and go to community college and then to a university. I'm a good student, with a 3.6 grade point average. I hope to get a scholarship based on that. I've been to the university here twice to visit. I really want to go there—possibly to study engineering or architecture. We'll see.

It's a problem not being able to speak English here. Twice I've run into Mexicans on the street who were having some kind of trouble, and I had to translate for them. I feel glad to know two languages. I had a friend here at school who could speak seven languages! He was from Ethiopia. I'd like to know that many languages someday, too.

I love to dance. I dance with a group that plays Latin music—merengue, salsa, banda, everything. We practice once a week. I think Americans like this dancing a lot, too. We've had a couple of really big dances with kids from schools all over Washington. I don't think I'll ever stop dancing.◆

Jorge is a Tarascan Indian from La Cumbre, Mexico. He and his uncle crossed the border with the help of a coyote. He lives in Nevada and is proud to be of Indian descent.

JORGE
I'M PROUD OF WHO I AM

My name is Jorge. I'm eighteen years old. I've been in the United States for a total of eight years. I remember the day I arrived in the United States. As soon as I got to my uncle's house in Los Angeles, he took me out to see the vineyards where he works and to see how things work. When we returned to the house the fireworks began exploding.

Two years later I moved to Nevada. There I met my mother for the first time since I was about three years old. My mother's been here about seventeen years. She came because my uncle was already here. He came when he was young. He was adopted by an American family and was able to get papers to work. I don't know

A Mixtec Indian family eats lunch while listening to a candidate give a speech before the 1994 Mexican national elections.

why I stayed behind in Mexico. Apparently, my mom and dad still argue about this. My mom always says it was my choice to stay or go, but how could a three-year-old decide something like that? The whole time I've been here, I've only lived with her for a year. We don't get along too well. I am angry because she left and because I never met my dad.

My grandparents raised me in La Cumbre. They taught me everything I know. We're Tarascan Indians. I was in denial back in those days about being an Indian. It was looked down on in my area. My grandfather always talked to me in Tarascan, but I only wanted to speak Spanish. In school you had to speak Spanish.

We lived on a reservation, but our family owned the land. We had a house in town that we could stay in when we had to go to town to get groceries or supplies. We'd load up the mules and walk about three hours and then shop and come back. I never understood why we never rode the mules to town and then walked them back.

We were in the pine-sap business. Pine sap is used to make windshields. My grandfather and I would take the barrels to town where they'd boil the sap and then lay it out in plastic sheets to form the windshields. You can also make glue from the sap. A lot of people here don't understand what that is all about. We use things differently down there—like cactus juice. In Mexico we used to drink it, and people here think that's really weird. Americans consider us poor when they hear these stories.

But we didn't consider ourselves poor. We lived in a beautiful open space. We had deer come to our door in the morning. We had goats and chickens. If we needed vegetables, we went out back and picked them. We grew corn and avocados. We had no need for the market except for things like shoes or seed. In the United States, everyone wraps up food and sticks it in the fridge. In Mexico you just add salt to meat and hang it up to dry.

We had no electricity. Our house was made of adobe, wood, and cement. Our kitchen floor was dirt, but you could still mop it and sweep it. The chimney was made of a mixture of mud, hay, and horse manure. Some kids here think that's gross. But it was warm inside when it was cold outside, and it was cool inside when it was hot outside. We didn't need any fans or electricity.

To get to the United States, we took a bus to Tijuana. My uncle, who lived in the United States, came to pick us up. We couldn't get papers so we decided to approach the guardpost. On the American side, there was a McDonald's and a supermarket. We decided to tell the guard that we just wanted to buy some food. He came out and told us to wait. He asked me if I was a *pollo* (chicken), or someone who wants to cross illegally. He asked my uncle if he was a coyote. We said no, we just wanted to try some American food to see what it was like. The guard said OK, and we snuck out the back of the supermarket. My other uncle was waiting in a truck, and he drove us to L.A.

I was really scared. From the American side I looked back, and you could see people waiting in the Mexican hills. After dark, the Mexicans all try to run across the border, and the guards try to catch them. If they catch you, they send you to jail, then deport you. If they catch you twice, you can go to jail for a long time. For a while when I was in L.A., I felt afraid every time I saw a cop.

Monica Cristal and her son Mauricio Lopez, residents of Mexico City, wear surgical masks to protect themselves from the city's heavy pollution.

A man from the Mexican state of Sinaloa trying to cross the border to the United States gives himself up to a U.S. border patrol agent.

My uncle brought me up here to Nevada to meet my mom. I'm not sure if it was supposed to be just a visit or permanent. The aunt that I had been living with was emotionally ill. She thought everyone was out to get her. She thought our neighbor was a witch. Beliefs like that are part of our culture. I was delivered by a *curandera*. That's someone who uses plants and herbs and rituals to heal people. There are lots of plants down there that cure pain—plants you make tea out of or plants you chew.

It was strange when I first met my mom. I was in the back of my uncle's van, waiting outside the house. All the neighborhood kids knew I was coming, and they were peering in the van's window at me. I felt like I was in the zoo. Finally my uncle came out and brought me inside.

I said to my mother, "Hi, how do you do?" I was so nervous. I didn't want to stay, but my uncle convinced me to give it a try. It was strange because even though we didn't get along, she didn't want me to leave.

Before I left Mexico I had a cousin who'd gone to the United States and come back. The first English word he taught me was a very bad one. But he said it meant "thank you" in English. I used to make up English in the mirror, jabbering away, so when I learned this new word I thought I was the coolest.

Later, in L.A., I was in court for stealing a car. I'd been spending time with some friends who had friends who were in gangs. It was my first time in court, and I was twelve. My uncle and his lawyer were with me. The judge was going to let me go since it was my first offense. I wanted to say "thank you." I bowed to him and said the bad word my cousin had taught me. The judge just looked at me in shock. He told us all to sit down again. He was talking at my lawyer really fast. He turned to me and told me that I was going to juvenile hall for two weeks for saying that. I told my lawyer I thought it meant "thank you." The judge said I should have known better but reduced my sentence to a week.

When I got home, my aunt was so mad. After that, I tried to learn English. I was in school, but I didn't have any records so I was two grades below where I should have been. It was hard to learn English because the neighborhood was Hispanic. Everyone spoke Spanish. It wasn't until I came to Reno that I learned English. I'm an average student now—mostly Bs, some As, some Cs. It is going to be very hard for me to get into college without a Social Security number.

I have friends whose parents own restaurants. I want to become that successful. I love to cook, and I want to study to be a chef. There are some really good programs around here, but I have a lot of obstacles to overcome. I'm trying, but everywhere I turn there's a wall. Somehow I've managed to survive. I have to thank my girlfriend and her aunt for letting me live here with them.

I have a son with my girlfriend Laurie. We're trying to get a day-care center going at our high school because it's really hard to study and watch a kid at the same time. Laurie goes to community college at night. She wants to take more classes, but she can't because I'm in school during the day. Right now we're living with Laurie's aunt. But her aunt works nights so she can't do too much babysitting.

I can't work because I'm illegal. When I was in L.A., I was working for my uncle picking grapes. That was good because I knew he wouldn't turn me in. I did that for a couple of years until I came here.

Recently, I changed my name back to my full Indian name. My mom was embarrassed about being Indian, but since I don't live with her anymore, I decided I wasn't ashamed. I'm proud of who I am.◆

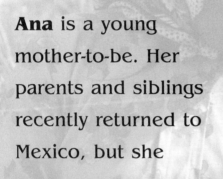

Ana is a young mother-to-be. Her parents and siblings recently returned to Mexico, but she stayed in the United States. She plans to marry her boyfriend and have her child here.

5 ANA
I'LL ALWAYS CARRY MEXICO INSIDE ME

My name is Ana, and I'm seventeen years old. I've been in the United States for four years. I come from Mexico City. I came to the United States with my parents and my three sisters. My dad wanted to bring us here to have a better life and education. My sisters are ten, thirteen, and fifteen years old. I have one brother who was born here. He's four.

In Mexico my dad was a carpenter. My mom used to sell food in a cafeteria for construction workers. When they came here, my dad started working in a restaurant as a dishwasher. Then he was a janitor. After that, he worked in a factory making window frames.

In Mexico, I worked in a bakery, selling pastries. My mom would make them. I started helping her when I was nine. Before that I used to take care of my little sisters.

We crossed the border with the help of our relatives who were already here. My uncle arranged it with someone in Mexico. We crossed at night. A coyote was watching out for the patrols. When it was clear, we could see a light blinking on the other side. It was a signal for us to run. After we crossed, we hid in the forest. We had to stay totally still and hidden. It was really hard for us to be quiet. My mom has asthma, so my dad had to carry her when we were running. There were some other Mexicans with us. About fifteen of us got in a car and went to a house where my uncle was waiting for us. That night we travelled to New Orleans.

My parents moved back to Mexico permanently four months ago. I stayed because I am pregnant. I wanted to stay here with my boyfriend Mario and finish high school. There are more opportunities here. But I miss my family so much. Every time I pass our old house, or where my dad used to work, I feel sad. I don't talk to them too often because it costs so much. But we write each other.

My parents left because we were having a lot of problems with one of my sisters, the fifteen-year-old. She was hanging around with gang members. My dad didn't want my other sisters to

A woman in a village in the Mexican state of Guerrero passes a graffiti-marked building. The graffiti calls for justice after the killings of eleven villagers by state security forces in 1995.

follow in her footsteps. So they all left, except me.

The whole family was beginning to separate. My father couldn't get my sister on the right path. One time he actually hit her, because he didn't want her to wear the gang clothes. He did it for her own good, so she wouldn't get herself killed. But she went to Child Protective Services and filed a complaint. My dad was taken out of the house. At the end he wasn't living with us. My mom didn't like that, and it seemed like it was going to take a long time for him to be able to come back. He was really sad.

49

My mom couldn't handle my sister alone. She was getting worse and worse. She did whatever she wanted. My younger sister was beginning to imitate her, and this scared my parents. So my dad finally just said, "This isn't working. I'd rather be with my family and work twice as hard than stay here."

I'm not involved in gangs. I used to be around them because of some of my friends, but they didn't interest me. For one thing, I'm more quiet than gang members are.

Right now I'm living with a friend. When my baby is born, Mario and I are going to get married.

When I'm done with school, I'd like to be a high school counselor. Sometimes it's hard for kids like my sister. She got kicked out of school and was told she couldn't come back. There aren't any programs for people like her. Or if there are, people don't know about them. I'd like to work with teens to help them figure out what they can do. It's going to take time.

The schools in Mexico are much more strict. There you don't have the same privileges as here. Everyone has to wear school uniforms, which is better. That way you can't be mistaken for a gang member.

Sometimes American people don't understand our culture. They just think we're different. That's true. We think in a different way. Some of us are more conservative. I find it easier to be friends with other Latinos. Here the school dances are

A Mexican woman and her son shop at a grocery store in Poughkeepsie, New York. The store caters to Mexican immigrants.

so different! So is the music people listen to, the way people dance, and the way boys and girls talk to each other. The Americans who are really involved in school and have great grades all stick together. There are some Americans who hang around with minorities.

Here it's much easier to earn money. In Mexico there aren't really jobs for young people. Here there are also more programs for teenagers. There are Hispanic groups that help you with food and clothes. That doesn't exist in Mexico.

I used to be in the marching band, playing the flute, but now that I'm pregnant, I can't do too much. I was also in the Union Latina, a group for

Many Mexicans who immigrate to the United States do so to escape their country's poverty. Above, an elderly couple in Mexico City begs for money in the city's main plaza.

Latino students. I used to play with my sister on a community soccer team.

Once I'm done with my education and I'm a wife and mother, I'd like to go back to visit my family in Mexico. But I won't stay there. The main thing is to get my papers first. That will happen when I marry Mario. We'll stay here, but I'll always carry Mexico inside me.◆

Dulce lives in Seattle. She plans to return to Mexico after she finishes high school. She is considering a career as a sculptor.

DULCE
I MISS MY FRIENDS

My name is Dulce. I've only been here seven months. I come from Mexico City. I'm sixteen years old. I came to the United States because I had the opportunity to study here and a chance to pursue things I might not be able to pursue in my own country. It was hard because I had to leave my family and parents. I'm here living with my aunt, my mother's sister. She's been here twenty years.

My aunt was always inviting me here, and I used to say, "OK, OK, I'll come." I was allowed to come when I was fifteen years old. I came for two months in the summer of 1994 on vacation, just to see what it was like. When I returned to Mexico, I told my parents that I liked it in the

United States, and they told me I could come back to study. So here I am.

I'll be here until I finish high school. I don't think I'll stay here forever. When I first arrived I couldn't speak English at all. I couldn't understand anything. It took me three months to learn the language and another three to feel really comfortable with it.

I'm studying all the usual subjects. At first I had bilingual classes. Now I also take the regular ones. Every night I study for two or three hours. I still have no idea what I want to do when I'm finished with school. People ask me all the time what I plan on doing, but I really don't know. I love sculpture and hope to pursue that. I've taken classes in sculpting in the past, but not recently because I have to study during the school year.

High school is so different here. I'm in the tenth grade. When I first got here, I was shocked by how different the people are. People would say things to me. I'd just respond yes or no because I wasn't even sure what they were saying. Plus I'd skipped a grade and was younger than everyone in my class. At first I didn't make many friends because no one in the bilingual class spoke English. Everybody was from different countries. But now I've made some American friends. Still, I find it hard to really communicate with them. Each ethnic group has its own cliques. They don't mix very often.

After school, I come home and hang out with my aunt and do things with my two cousins, who are seven and twelve. I love to play all sports and do aerobics. My favorite subject is biology, but I don't want to be a doctor! I can't stand blood.

In Mexico, I always played sports after school with my friends. If not, I'd go to the library, since we always had tons of homework. In Mexico I was studying geography, which they don't have at my school here. But in Mexico, we didn't have science classes like here.

I have two brothers and two sisters. I'm the fourth child, the youngest of the girls. My sisters are all grown and working. My parents live in Georgia now. My father is a construction engineer. He's studying American building techniques. They'll be returning to Mexico soon. But first they're going to visit me here for a month.

What I love about Seattle is the environment. But it's more dangerous here than in Mexico. It's dangerous in the streets and in the schools. There isn't as much security in the schools here. Also, the students here are much more aggressive, I think.

My older sister came here to study for her junior year. She stayed here for four years. She speaks very good English now and uses it in her work. She works in the tourism industry in Mexico City. I'd like to use English someday as well—that's the reason I'm doing all this.

The culture here is very different. Everyone has their own ideas. The people know a lot more about the world and other things than people do in Mexico. In Mexico City, though, the people are fairly well educated because of the universities.

Families here seem to spend a lot of time together until the kids are about fourteen or fifteen years old. Then everyone starts to leave. In Mexico it's the opposite. The kids aren't around when they're young, but end up coming back and spending more time with their families as adults. Divorces are also much more common here. It almost never happens in Mexico.

I've seen lots of racism in the schools here, even between Mexicans. Some of them want to act like they're better than others. If they've been here a long time they say, "I'm from here." They want to be considered a part of this culture.

I have some really great teachers here. In general, adults in the United States seem to pay more attention to kids. They have more patience for teaching us.

Teens here have a lot more freedom. At home I can go out to hear music or something if I really want to. But my parents always prefer me to stay home with them. If I do go, the very latest I can stay out is 11 PM. I didn't start thinking about going out until I was fourteen or fifteen. Here kids start going out at night when they are much younger.

I miss my friends in Mexico a lot. We write to each other, but I still miss them. I hope I can visit them before I return for good, just to see how everything's going.◆

Glossary

Bering Strait A fifty-six-mile-wide passageway separating northern Asia from North America.

bustling Noisy, lively.

colonialism Control of a people by a foreign power.

compelling Forceful, convincing.

coyote One who smuggles immigrants into the United States.

diversity Variety.

falter To move unsteadily; to waver.

free trade The exchange of goods between countries without restrictions.

innovative New, groundbreaking, imaginative.

nomads People who have no fixed home but move from place to place.

peninsula Land surrounded by water on three sides.

potential Possibility of future growth or change.

rampant Unchecked, unrestrained.

refugee A person who flees to a foreign country to escape unfavorable conditions in his or her homeland.

regress To move backwards to an earlier, worse time.

stability State of calm; freedom from unrest.

For Further Reading

Ashabranner, Brent. *The Vanishing Border: A Photographic Journey Along Our Border with Mexico.* New York: Putnam, 1987.

Brimner, Larry Dane. *A Migrant Family.* Minneapolis: Lerner, 1992.

Carlson, Lori M. *Cool Salsa: Bilingual Poems on Growing Up Hispanic in the United States.* New York: Henry Holt, 1995.

Cockcroft, James D. *Outlaws in the Promised Land: Mexican Immigrant Workers and America's Future.* New York: Bantam, 1991.

Hoobler, Dorothy, and Thomas Hoobler. *The Mexican American Family Album.* New York: Oxford University Press, 1994.

Index

About the Author

Gerry Hadden is a writer and musician who lives in Seattle, Washington. He is the author of *Teenage Refugees From Guatemala Speak Out* and coauthor of *Home Tree Home* (Penguin). He is also a reporter and news anchor for KPLU, a National Public Radio station.

Photo Credits

Cover, Michele and Tom Grimm/International Stock; pp. 6, 11, 21, 27, 41, 42, 49, 52, AP/Wide World Photos; p. 8, Bill Mitchell/Archive Photos; pp. 12, 34, UPI/Corbis-Bettmann; pp. 16, 19, Reuters/John Gibbons; pp. 24, 36, 46, 54, Buddy Mays/International Stock; p. 29, Slobodan Dimitron/Impact Visuals; pp. 30, 51, Jack Kurtz/Impact Visuals; p. 32, Cindy Reiman/Impact Visuals; p. 38, Thor Swift/Impact Visuals.

Layout and Design

Kim Sonsky